CLEMENT C. MOORE

The Night Before
CHRISTMAS

Emma Gober
Leland, Ill.

ILLUSTRATED BY CYNDY SZEKERES

GOLDEN BOOKS • NEW YORK
Western Publishing Company, Inc. Racine, Wisconsin 53404

'Twas the night before Christmas

when all through the house,
Not a creature was stirring,
    not even a mouse.
The stockings were hung
    by the chimney with care,
In hopes that St. Nicholas
    soon would be there.

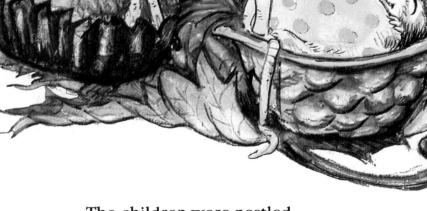

The children were nestled
all snug in their beds,
While visions of sugarplums
danced in their heads;

And Mama in her kerchief,
and I in my cap,
Had just settled our brains
for a long winter's nap,

When out on the lawn
    there arose such a clatter,
I sprang from my bed
    to see what was the matter.

Away to the window
I flew like a flash,
Tore open the shutters
and threw up the sash.

The moon on the breast of the new-fallen snow
Gave the luster of midday to objects below,
When what to my wondering eyes should appear
But a miniature sleigh and eight tiny reindeer,
With a little old driver so lively and quick
I knew in a moment it must be St. Nick.

More rapid than eagles his coursers they came,
And he whistled and shouted and called them by name:
"Now Dasher! Now Dancer! Now Prancer and Vixen!
On Comet! On Cupid! On Donder and Blitzen!
To the top of the porch! To the top of the wall!
Now dash away, dash away, dash away all!"

As dry leaves that before the wild hurricane fly,
When they meet with an obstacle, mount to the sky,
So up to the house-top the coursers they flew,
With a sleigh full of toys and St. Nicholas, too.

And then in a twinkling I heard on the roof
The prancing and pawing of each little hoof.
As I drew in my head and was turning around,

Down the chimney St. Nicholas came with a bound.
He was dressed all in fur from his head to his foot,
And his clothes were all tarnished with ashes and soot.
A bundle of toys he had flung on his back,
And he looked like a peddler just opening his pack.

His eyes, how they twinkled!
His dimples, how merry!
His cheeks were like roses,
his nose like a cherry!

His droll little mouth
was drawn up like a bow,
And the beard on his chin was as white as the snow.

The stump of a pipe
   he held tight in his teeth,
And the smoke
   it encircled his head like a wreath.

He had a broad face and a little round belly
That shook when he laughed like a bowlful of jelly.
He was chubby and plump, a right jolly old elf,
And I laughed when I saw him, in spite of myself.
A wink of his eye and a twist of his head
Soon gave me to know I had nothing to dread.

He spoke not a word but went straight to his work,
And filled all the stockings, then turned with a jerk,
And laying his finger aside of his nose
And giving a nod, up the chimney he rose.

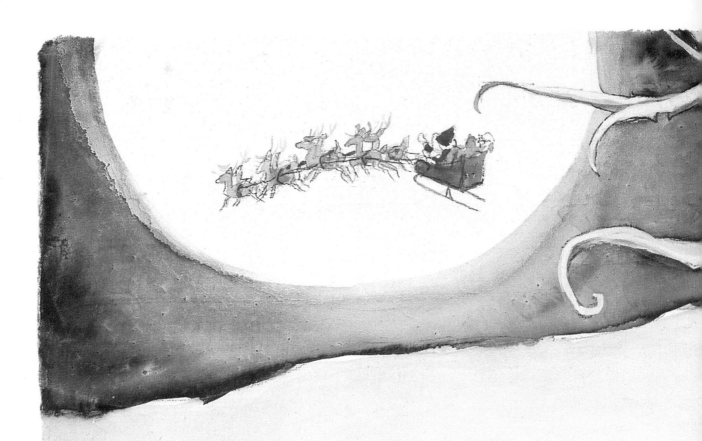

He sprang to his sleigh, to his team gave a whistle,
And away they all flew like the down of a thistle.
But I heard him exclaim ere he drove out of sight:

"Happy Christmas to all,
And to all a good night!"